MICHAEL DAHL'S
REALLY SCARY STORIES

Michael Dahl's Really Scary Stories
are published by Stone Arch Books
A Capstone Imprint
1710 Roe Crest Drive
North Mankato, Minnesota 56003
www.mycapstone.com

Library of Congress Cataloging-in-Publication Data is available on
the Library of Congress website.

ISBN: 978-1-4965-3774-4 (library binding)
ISBN: 978-1-4965-3778-2 (ebook PDF)

Summary: Siblings Kareem and Amina are dreading a night with their
babysitter, Mrs. Heeley. The only good thing is, she always brings
cupcakes. But when they go to get a tasty treat, Kareem and Amina
find that the cupcakes seem to be devouring one another. Will Kareem
and Amina be able to stop the madness before the zombie cupcakes
take over? This collection of scary stories will bring you the
answer to that question and many others, but you may never want a
cupcake again!

Designer: Hilary Wacholz
Image Credits: Dmitry Natashin

Printed in Canada.
032016   009647F16

ZOMBIE CUPCAKES
AND OTHER SCARY TALES

By Michael Dahl

Illustrated by
Xavier Bonet

STONE ARCH BOOKS
a capstone imprint

TABLE OF
CONTENTS

Up and down and around again the train rocketed along the track. "What's that?" screamed Annie, pointing ahead of them.

Mia was too startled to speak or move. Who was her real mother? She couldn't remember what her mother was wearing when they had arrived at the store.

Kareem was about to laugh, but his eye caught a glimpse of the torn apart cakes again. The insides were gone. Licked clean. The way a zombie ate brains.

Dear Reader,

When we were young, my cousin Randy was terrified of scary movies.

Whenever we went to the old movie theater in his small town of Fairmont, Minnesota, there would often be trailers for upcoming scary films.

If creepy music came on at the start of the trailer, Randy would close his eyes, duck behind the seat in front of him, and sit on the floor. And you know what floors are like at movie theaters!

Even though Randy refused to watch the frightening images on the big screen, he asked me to describe exactly what was happening. He didn't want to be left out, and hearing about it was not as scary as watching it.

Maybe as you read the scary stories in this book, you won't be as terrified as if you actually observed them. Maybe. When there are monsters and ghosts and strange sounds involved, I can't make any **PROMISES** . . .

Michael Dahl

WHAT THEY
FOUND IN
THE ALLEY

Cars from the nearby streets have gone silent. There are no chirping birds. No rumbling planes overhead. No humming of machinery or workers' voices from inside the warehouse. It feels wrong to him. He realizes he can't even hear his feet scraping against the ground.

Chip can't even hear himself breathing. He feels like he's inside a giant aquarium.

As he trots along, the silence and the darkness grow deeper and deeper.

When he reaches the end of the alley, Chip feels different. But he doesn't have time to think about it. He hears the bell ringing outside the school, and he knows that he needs to get to class!

He runs to his science class and plops down in his assigned seat. He made it just in time!

During class, Chip is quiet and listens to the teacher, which is something he does not do every day.

After class, the teacher, Mr. Salah, asks Chip to stay behind for a minute. Chip stands obediently as Mr. Salah returns to his desk.

"Chip," says Mr. Salah, "are you feeling okay this morning?"

"Yes," says Chip.

"Is everything all right at home?" asks Mr. Salah gently.

"Yes," says Chip.

Mr. Salah smiles. "It seems as if something may be bothering you, Chip. You're normally not this quiet in class, you know." Mr. Salah tries to make it sound like a joke.

"Sorry," says Chip.

"Nothing to be sorry for, Chip," says Mr. Salah. "Some days we don't feel like ourselves. It happens to everyone. Sometimes we get up on the wrong side of the bed. Or we change our routine."

Chip looks up at the teacher. Mr. Salah is a bit startled. The boy's eyes look dark and empty.

"The alley," says Chip.

Mr. Salah is confused. "Alley?"

"I took a short cut through the alley."

"I see," says the teacher. "Do you always go through the alley?"

Chip shakes his head slowly. Then he says, "I found something there."

Mr. Salah leans forward. "Oh? What did you find?"

The boy lowers his eyes and remains silent.

The teacher sits back in his chair and waits. Chip won't talk.

"All right, Chip," he says. "You can go. But let me know if there's anything you need help with."

"Okay," says Chip. He picks up the books on his desk, opens the door, and then walks out.

As the door closes behind Chip, Mr. Salah shakes his head. He is puzzled by the boy's strange behavior. He walks over to the classroom windows and gazes across the school parking lot toward the huge, sprawling warehouses. If he stares hard enough, Mr. Salah can just make out the entrance to the alley.

He's heard strange stories about that alley, but there's no way they could be true. The biggest rumor is that the alley has a portal to an alien realm, but not everyone is picked to enter the portal.

Once the last school bus has left, Mr. Salah grabs his own backpack and walks toward the alley.

The look in Chip's eyes has been bothering him all day. Mr. Salah is also bothered by what the boy said. What did he find in the alley?

The teacher hesitates at the entrance to the alley. It is quiet, and the shadows creep up the walls as the sun slides lower in the sky. Mr. Salah checks his watch. He is going to time how long it takes to walk through the alley. He takes his first step. It is only a matter of minutes until he is deep inside the alley. The sound of his footsteps grows quieter the farther he goes.

It is getting dark. There is no one near the entrance to the alley. No one to see the burst of red light. No one to hear a voice cry out suddenly and then stop.

Chip is nowhere near the alley. He doesn't see the burst of light or hear the cry. But he doesn't have to. He knows what happens to Mr. Salah. He knows what the man found. Or rather, he knows what found him. The same thing that Chip found.

Chip is in his bedroom now. It is late and time for bed. Once he closes the door, he goes to sit down on the bed. He puts his hands on his ears, then he carefully unscrews his head from his neck. The boy gently places the head beside him on the covers. He reaches inside his neck and pulls out a long, thin antenna.

The antenna begins to hum. A voice crackles through the air in Chip's bedroom.

"Replacement robot of young humanoid reporting. All clear. Repeat, all clear. The invasion may now proceed to Phase Two."

THE CREEPING WOMAN

That evening after Christmas Eve dinner, the Hamilton family celebrated a tradition that eleven-year old Jawan always looked forward to. They told scary stories before they went to bed, before the long, deep night when Santa Claus would bring their gifts.

Five-year old Reesha didn't seem to mind the spooky tales of ghosts and zombies and bumps in the night. All she could think of was presents. She stared at their small fireplace, worried that Santa wouldn't fit down the chimney.

"Santa will find a way in," Mrs. Hamilton reassured her. "He always does."

"Don't worry, Reesha," Jawan said. "Santa is magic. He'll figure out how to get in using the fireplace, no matter what size it is."

"Fireplaces remind me of another story," said Mr. Hamilton. He made everyone gasp with his whispered tale about a phantom face that could be seen in a roaring fire. At the end of the story, he shouted out a loud "Boo!" and grabbed Reesha. Everyone screamed and then laughed. Then the Hamilton children all got ready for bed. Jawan and his brother Drew were walking up the stairs to their bedroom when Shonda, their older sister, hurried past them.

"You better look out for the Creeping Woman," she said.

"What's that?" asked Jawan.

"You haven't heard about her?" Shonda asked, surprised.

"It's just one of those things," said Drew. "You know, a legend."

"It may be a legend," said Shonda, "but it's true. I even heard it on the news tonight."

"You did not!" said Drew.

"Ask Dad," said his sister. She turned her attention to Jawan. "A woman has been seen creeping around houses at night. Sometimes she walks hunched over, like her back is broken. And sometimes she walks on all fours. Like a dog or coyote."

"In the snow?" cried Drew.

"Why does she do that?" asked Jawan, his eyes wide and his skin prickling with fear.

"I don't know," said Shonda. "Maybe to steal Christmas presents?"

"Yeah, right," Drew said. "Or to eat people. Ha!"

"It was on the news," said Shonda. "The creeping woman is out there in the dark." She grinned at them and then scurried to her room and shut the door.

Drew rolled his eyes. "She's a big fat liar," he said to his brother. "It's just another scary story."

"You don't think there's a real woman out there?" asked Jawan.

"Nah, and if there is, we'll just run away," said

Drew. "She can't move fast if she's crawling around. And no one's getting my presents!"

The boys settled down in their beds, one on either side of the small room.

Jawan frowned. He sat up and looked at the bedroom door. "Is the front door locked?" he asked.

Drew yawned. "Dad always locks it. Stop worrying."

Jawan lay back down and turned to stare out the window. A streetlight illuminated the falling snow, turning it to glittering diamonds streaming past the window. *There couldn't be a woman crawling out in the snow*, thought Jawan. *She'd be frozen.* He thought about the front door again. Had his father locked it? What about the door to the garage? Maybe he should get up and check. But as Jawan continued to watch the sparkling snow, his bed grew warmer and more comfortable, and soon he fell asleep.

Jawan wasn't the only member of the family worried about doors. Little Reesha thought about them too. She was still worried that Santa might not be able to come inside and leave her presents. After the lights were turned out and everyone had gone to sleep, the little girl crept down the carpeted stairs. Reesha made her way through the living room. She tiptoed past the Christmas tree, past the fireplace, past the coatrack, and walked to the front door.

"Santa can come this way," she said to herself.

She reached for the doorknob, but before she unlocked it, she heard a sound. Something was scratching on the outside of the door.

Reesha smiled. "Santa!" she whispered.

The little girl unlocked the door and pulled it open. She watched, frozen, as an arm reached around the bottom of the door and a woman crawled inside the house. A woman with long, snow-white hair and diamond-bright eyes that glittered with hunger.

PLEASE DON'T TOUCH THE BUS DRIVER

Grace kept hoping that her grandmother wouldn't say anything embarrassing during their trip to the museum.

Too late.

They hadn't even reached the museum when it happened. In fact, they were standing at the bus stop only two blocks from Grandmother's house when the old woman looked around at the commuters and snorted. Grace's grandmother always made that sound right before she said something terrible.

"People don't look you in the face anymore," said her grandmother. Grace thought her voice was much too loud. "Everyone's gawking at their little screen-things."

Screen things. She means phones or tablets, Grace thought.

"People used to talk to each other," her grandmother continued. "You used to stand here on the sidewalk and have an actual conversation with your neighbors. Using words. Out loud. Not anymore. Not when they've got their faces buried in those little Google-machines."

Grace's grandmother had once caught her working on her laptop at home. That's when the older woman first heard of Google. Now every device was a Google-machine. Grace squirmed, hoping that no one else at the bus stop was listening.

Then another snort.

"Even if you did want to talk," said her grandmother, "people can't hear you because they all wear those little ear plugs."

"They're called earbuds, Grandma," said Grace.

"Huh?" said the old woman.

"They're earbuds," Grace said patiently.

"Ear pumps?"

Buds, like buds on a tree," said Grace. "That's what they sort of look like."

"A stupid name for a stupid thing," said her grandmother. "Please tell me you'll never wear that kind of contraption, Grace."

Grace didn't know how to answer. She had earbuds in her backpack right now, in fact, coiled up next to her iPad. Luckily, a bus came into view at that moment.

"The bus," she said. Grace couldn't wait until they arrived at the museum. Maybe if her grandmother were surrounded by old stuff, like paintings and statues, she wouldn't feel so cranky.

"People don't hear a thing you say anymore." Her grandmother didn't show any signs of calming down. "It's rude, that's what it is. Downright rude!"

The bus halted and the door opened with a hiss.

"Rude!" the old woman repeated.

The bus driver was a young man with long black hair and big ears. As passengers climbed onto the bus, he just stared out the big front window and swayed his head back and forth. He was wearing earbuds. Grace felt sick to her stomach.

Please, please, please don't say anything, the girl kept repeating in her mind.

Grandmother climbed to the top of the steps. She gave one look at the young bus driver and snorted. "Young man," she said.

"What's wrong, Grandma?" asked Grace, quickly stepping up next to her.

"How does he know where to stop if he can't hear me?" she exclaimed. She turned to the driver again. "Young man!"

Grace glanced at the other passengers. They were all staring at her grandmother and two or three were staring to mumble. The bus driver closed the door, revved the engine, and pulled away from the curb. Grandmother held on to a metal pole, but would not sit down.

"Young man, can you hear me?" she said. She put her face inches from his head.

The bus driver ignored her. *His music must be really loud,* thought Grace.

"This is ridiculous!" said her grandmother. She reached out and grasped the cord of the earbuds that lay resting on the driver's chest. She pulled, and the buds popped out of both ears. With a triumphant smile, the old woman began, "Now, will you listen —"

Her voice was drowned out by a loud hissing sound. It was not the bus door. It reminded Grace of air escaping from a balloon.

Grandmother screamed and fell back into an empty seat.

The hiss was coming from the ears of the young driver. Grace stared, speechless, as the man collapsed into himself. His head sank onto his neck, his chest caved in, and his hands shrank and dropped off of the steering wheel. His legs shriveled up and hung from the seat like deflated balloons.

The driver's seat was quickly covered with a blob of empty skin.

"Help! Do something!" the old woman yelled. Only Grace heard her. All the other passengers were busy listening to their earbuds or staring at their little screens.

ROLLER GHOSTER

Ricky and Oscar couldn't remember how many times they'd ridden the roller coaster that weekend.

"Best. Ride. Ever!" said Ricky.

"That was awesome!" said Oscar.

The Killer Comet roller coaster inside the Richdale shopping mall was one of the fastest in the world. The twisting, plunging track was less than a mile long, but at one dramatic drop, nicknamed the Dark Star, it reached a speed of 150 miles per hour. The speed was what drew such long lines to the ride. The speed was also responsible for the ride's one deadly accident.

"Have you heard about the ghost on this ride?" said a boy to his girlfriend. They were standing in line ahead of Ricky and Oscar. The girl shook her head. "A kid died," he said. "He jumped off or was thrown off at the Dark Star drop. And some people say they see him still riding it."

The girl gasped.

Oscar rolled his eyes. He and Ricky had been hearing this story for years. It didn't stop them from riding the Killer Comet whenever they had a chance.

In less than ten minutes, they were boarding the roller coaster. The couple sat just in front of them in the same car. The outside of each car was built to look like a small rocket. A blazing golden number was painted on the front.

"Uh oh, Annie," said the boy in front of them. "We got Car Thirteen."

"Stop it, Ryan," said Annie. "I'm only going on this once, and that's it. Don't make it even harder for me."

"But thirteen is an unlucky number . . ." Ryan continued.

"I said stop, Ryan, or I'm getting off!"

"Too late," he said.

The safety bars came down, locking everyone into their seats. Ricky and Oscar were so used to the ride that they never even held on to the bar anymore. In front of them, Annie gripped the bar with white knuckles.

"And we're off!" shouted Oscar.

A powerful cable under the track pulled the train of cars up, up, up toward the first and tallest peak.

"I can't look!" wailed Annie.

The train slowly crested the peak, and then swiftly, almost without warning, it plunged down the steep slope, accompanied by passengers' screams and cries and laughter. Up and down and around again the train rocketed along the track.

"What's that?" screamed Annie, pointing ahead of them.

The roller coaster track seemed almost vertical as it plunged inside a fake mountainside covered with trolls and ogres.

"That's the Dark Star," said Ryan. "Hold on!"

"Ooh!" said Oscar, holding his arms up over his head. "Watch out for the ghoooooost!"

The air seemed to rush out of their bodies as the train shot inside the mountain. Blackness swallowed up the cars. There was silence during this part of the ride. Passengers were too scared to scream.

Then, finally, the slope became more gradual and the train began to slow.

"Smile!" shouted Ryan.

In a few moments, the ride was over. Passengers were laughing and shouting and jumping out of the cars.

"Let's stop over by the photo booth," said Ricky, grinning, to his friend.

They followed close behind Ryan and Annie as the couple made their way to the booth near the foot of the roller coaster.

There was a camera that snapped pictures of each car as it plunged into the Dark Star. For a few dollars, people could buy the photos.

Ryan and Annie looked at their photo as it came up on the big display screen.

"Ha! There we are," said Ryan.

"I look like a scared cat," Annie said, laughing.

Ryan gripped Annie's arm. "Wait," he said. "Those two kids behind us."

"What two kids?" said Annie.

Ryan pointed. "See those two boys sitting in the seat behind us?"

"That seat was empty," said Annie.

"That seat's always empty," said the redheaded man running the photo booth. "That's Car Thirteen. That's the car the two kids fell out of twenty years ago."

The photo of Ryan and Annie showed the outlines of two boys sitting directly behind them. Their faces could barely be seen, but it looked as if they were laughing.

"I want to go home," said Annie.

Oscar and Ricky chuckled as they watched the couple hurry out of the park.

"Want to go again?" asked Oscar.

"I'm dying to," said Ricky with a smile.

MOTHER WHO

There are just too many, thought Mia. *Way too many!*

"You have to choose one, Mia," said her mother. "Only one."

Mia was staring at the cereal boxes stacked on the shelves in front of her. There had to be twenty or thirty different brands. Each one was packaged in a colorful box with a cute name and an even cuter cartoon character.

"Hurry up, Mia," said her mother. "I have a lot more items on my list." The woman tightened her grip on the shopping cart, wheeled down the aisle, and then disappeared around the corner. "Just one!" her mother called out.

I give up, Mia thought. How could she choose

between *Kiddy Bits* or *Chock o' Chocolate* or *Pretty Pony Puffs?*

Mia's family wasn't poor, but her mom was always careful with money. When they went to the store, it was always the same: one brand of cereal, one brand of juice, one brand of cheese. Mia decided she needed more flavors in her life. Which is exactly what it said on the *Kiddy Bits* box: "Taste every flavor in every bite!"

So Mia stopped thinking and started grabbing. *We can afford it,* she decided.

She ended up with five different brands — the most she could carry at one time. Then she headed down the aisle and saw her mother wheel into sight with her cart.

"There you are, Mia," her mother exclaimed. "What took you so long?"

Mia was about to answer when she heard a familiar voice behind her. "Mia!"

She turned and saw her mother with the shopping cart at the other end of the aisle.

"Hurry up!" said the second mother. "We have to run to the pharmacy after this."

"Mia, what are you standing there for?" asked the first mother.

Bang! Another shopper's cart bumped into her mother's — the first mother's — cart. "Sorry!" said the shopper. When the shopper came into view, Mia saw that it was another woman who looked exactly like her mother. In fact, all three women looked exactly like each other, but they wore different clothes.

One wore jeans and black sandals, another wore a flowery skirt and scarf, and the third was in dressy slacks and a sweater with a colorful headband. Their carts were full of different items. But none of them seemed to notice that they were exact copies of one another.

Mia was too startled to speak or move. Who was her real mother? She couldn't remember what her mother was wearing when they had arrived at the store.

Mia cried out, "Mom!"

"Yes, honey?" the trio called together.

Too many, thought Mia. *How do I choose?*

The girl dropped her cereal boxes and ran toward the end of the aisle, the end where only one of her mothers stood, the one wearing the flowery skirt. As she ran past the cart, the woman called out, "Mia! Where do you think you're going?" She reached out to Mia, but the girl was too quick.

A voice rang out over the store loudspeaker. "Clean up in aisle six. Cereal boxes down."

A moment later, Mia stood outside in the parking lot, stopping to catch her breath. Her hands were shaking. She wanted to go home. She wanted her mother. But *which* mother?

Tears began to flood Mia's eyes. *How did this happen?* Mia wondered. She had just been standing in the aisle, trying to decide which cereal to choose when — that was it! She had wanted more than one box of cereal. Did some part of her also want more than one mother? Had she caused her mother to turn into three different versions?

If I think hard enough, maybe the clones will disappear and only my real mom will remain, Mia thought. *With her one brand of milk, one brand of soft drink, one day a week to do any*

type of shopping, and always at the same boring
stores . . .

But maybe there was another choice. One of the other two mothers might be more fun. Someone who laughed and shopped and loved spending money on her wonderful daughter. A happy mother, who was more easy-going.

Mia thought hard. She tried picturing the kind of mother she really wanted.

Concentrating was hard work. Mia dashed away from the doors and into the parking lot to find their car. She would wait there for her mother, one mother, to come and drive them both home. On her way to the parking lot, Mia wondered if she'd find three blue SUVs in a row, all with the same license plate.

But the car stood alone. Her mom's blue SUV was where they'd parked it. Mia knew the doors would be locked. But the sun was shining and the air was warm, so she decided to stand around and wait.

Mia kept her eye on the store's front doors.

There! Her mother was leaving the store, pushing the cart. And there was only one!

Yes! she thought. *Finally.*

Mia leaned back against the car and smiled. She closed her eyes, letting the sun warm her face.

"Mia," came her mother's voice. "Why did you grab five cereal boxes?"

Mia opened her eyes. The SUV was surrounded by fourteen or fifteen women who all looked alike. Each one stood behind a shopping cart filled with grocery bags. Each one stared at Mia.

"I told you to pick just one," said all the mothers at once. "Now you've gone and made it harder."

The circle of women tightened around Mia and the car. They stepped closer and closer.

"Pick one, Mia!" they chanted. "Pick one! Pick one! Pick ONE!

ZOMBIE CUPCAKES

Everything about Old Mrs. Heeley was odd. Her clothes were odd and old-fashioned. Her gray hair was squeezed into a lacey hairnet, her plastic glasses hung from a chain around her neck, and she wore mismatched shoes that gave her a limp when she walked.

Mr. and Mrs. Harper had lined up a different babysitter for that evening, but the sitter had come down with the flu. After several more phone calls, the only person available was Mrs. Heeley. She said she'd love to help out. She loved sweet young children.

Thankfully, there was something about the old woman that Kareem and Amina both liked. She brought a tray of homemade cupcakes with her.

The cupcakes were fresh. They smelled of chocolate and raspberry, of lemon and red velvet cake.

"They're my favorite thing to bake," Mrs. Heeley had said when she arrived. She passed the tray to Mr. Harper and smiled at the children. "And I know sweet children like sweet things to eat."

"Right you are, Mrs. Heeley," Mr. Harper said. "And thank you. I'll just put them in the breadbox so they don't get stale."

Soon, Mr. and Mrs. Harper left.

Mrs. Heeley had insisted that the kids wait until after dinner to eat the cupcakes. But when dinner was over, she suggested that the children relax a while in front of the TV.

"What *is* that show you two are watching?" asked Mrs. Heeley.

Amina waved her hand. "It's just about zombies," she said.

"Zombies!" said Mrs. Heeley, startled. "That doesn't sound like a good show for children," said the old woman.

"It's okay," said Kareem. "Our parents let us watch it."

"Zombies aren't real," explained Amina. "It's all pretend."

"Pretend . . ." echoed Mrs. Heeley.

"Amina doesn't have to worry about becoming a zombie," said Kareem. "Zombies like to eat brains, and Amina doesn't have any!"

"Hmm, eating brains doesn't sound very tempting," said Mrs. Heeley.

"Hey, look!" cried Kareem. "There's a zombie eating brains now."

The two children stared at the screen, while Mrs. Heeley returned to her crossword puzzle, tsk-tsking under her breath.

"That reminds me," said Kareem. "Can we have cupcakes now?"

"Please?" begged Amina.

"Yes, I think it's time," Mrs. Heeley said.

Kareem raced into the kitchen ahead of Amina and opened the breadbox. He froze. "What's wrong with the cupcakes?" he whispered.

Crumbs and clumps of cake were scattered throughout the box and all over the kitchen counter. Quickly, he counted. Eight cupcakes. Eight! Mrs. Heeley had brought over sixteen. Four for each member of the Harper family. What had happened?

He peered at the remains of the cupcakes. They looked torn in half. The insides, the wonderful fillings that had smelled so delicious, were gone. As if they had been scooped out.

"What did you do to the cupcakes?" yelled Amina. She walked up behind Kareem. "You ruined them!"

"I didn't do it," said Kareem.

"Only two at the most," called Mrs. Heeley from the other room. "Save the rest for tomorrow."

"Something's wrong with them," cried Amina.

"Wrong?"

Old Mrs. Heeley limped into the kitchen and made her way to the counter. She stared at the breadbox.

"What did you children do?" she exclaimed.

"Nothing," said Kareem. He explained that the mess was exactly how it looked when he opened the breadbox.

"Well," said Mrs. Heeley, "cupcakes don't just fall apart like that. Or disappear."

"Maybe zombies got them," said Amina.

"Or maybe some children snuck in here while I wasn't watching," said the old woman.

Kareem and Amina protested, but Mrs. Heeley was having none of it. She said it was time for bed and no arguing.

But before they left the kitchen, and while the woman's back was turned, Kareem grabbed a cupcake with thick chocolate frosting. In his bedroom he bit into the dark cake and his tongue discovered a creamy glob of tart raspberry jam. It was delicious.

Lying in bed later that night, Kareem gazed at the shadows of tree branches on his bedroom ceiling. The image of the torn cupcakes kept spinning through his brain. Did mice get into the cupcakes? A hungry robber? Aliens? Ghosts?

Kareem heard a noise. He climbed out of bed and cracked open his door. Something, or someone, was moving through the house. He heard a faint *ping*, then another. Whatever it was, the sounds were coming from the kitchen.

Kareem snuck down the hallway. Mrs. Harper left the small light above the oven on every night, so Kareem could see clearly enough in the dim, empty room. He could hear Mrs. Heeley snoring in the living room, and he was careful not to make a sound.

Scritch, scratch . . .

The noise was coming from the breadbox.

So it was *mice!* Kareem hated mice. He grabbed a wooden spoon from a nearby holder and held it over his head. With his other hand, he slowly reached for the plastic knob on the breadbox lid. With a flick of his hand, he flipped it open.

No tails. No whiskers. Nothing squeaking. But there was movement. The cupcakes were on their sides, rocking back and forth ever so slightly. It was as if someone had shaken the breadbox and then suddenly stopped. Kareem counted them. Only five full cupcakes. More of them were torn apart and their soft insides had been scooped out.

Kareem picked up one of the full cakes. It looked puffier than before. Bigger. The frosting was brighter, too, with three different colors of icing mixed together.

"I knew it was you!" Kareem spun around and saw his sister watching him, her arms folded.

"No, no," said Kareem. "I just got here. Look." He held out the cupcake to her. "Does this look bigger to you?"

"Bigger?" Amina made a face. "You mean fatter? I don't know. Hey, what happened to the other ones?"

Kareem shrugged. The brother and sister stood side by side, surveying the breadbox and the cakey mess.

"The fat ones *are* fatter, I think," said Amina. "Do you think they've been eating up the other ones?"

Kareem was about to laugh, but his eye caught a glimpse of the torn apart cakes again.

The insides were gone. Licked clean. The way a zombie ate brains.

"Okay, this is nuts!" said Kareem. "You've been eating them!"

"I didn't do it," said Amina, pouting. "You did it, and you're trying to blame me."

Kareem shook his head. "I'm going to bed. And so are you. We'll figure this out in the morning."

Amina didn't argue. She closed the breadbox and followed her brother out of the kitchen.

Before she walked down the hall to her bedroom, Amina stopped. "If they are zombie cupcakes," she whispered, "think what would have happened if we ate one."

"What do you mean?" said Kareem, worried.

Amina shuddered. "We would have turned into one of them. The living dead!" she said.

Kareem shook his head. "I eat French fries all the time," he said. "Do I look like a French fry? Have any French fries eaten me? Go to bed, Amina."

Kareem watched her go into her bedroom and shut the door. He was still worried. He raced back to the kitchen, convinced it was mice or some other animal. And he would wait all night until he caught them.

As he entered the kitchen, he heard a squeak. A tiny cry of pain. The sound sent goose bumps up and down his neck. He opened the breadbox and saw only two cupcakes left. More crumbs were scattered around them. But no frosting. He hadn't realized that the first time. No blobs of sugary icing or creamy insides. Only cake crumbs. So where did the frosting go?

Carefully, Kareem picked up the two remaining cupcakes. He hurried back to his room and set them on top of his dresser. He planned to watch them all night.

If a human ate a zombie cupcake, what would happen to them? Would they become a zombie too? Is that a new way for someone to become a member of the living dead? *I only ate one,* he thought. *Only one.*

As it grew late, Kareem's eyes drooped and he started dreaming. Cupcakes and zombies . . .

The next morning, Kareem jumped out of bed and ran to his mirror. He looked the same. No signs of cake or frosting. He was still human. He laughed at how scared he had felt. Then he checked his dresser.

The cupcakes were gone.

Kareem rushed to the kitchen. He was going to tell his parents what had happened the night before, but when he walked through the kitchen doorway, he was startled to find Old Mrs. Heeley hunched over the stove.

"Oh, hi, sweetie," she said.

Kareem was confused. "Where are Mom and Dad?" he asked.

Mrs. Heeley wiped her hands on a towel hanging from the stove. "Well, your dad's at work," she said. "And your mom forgot she had to see the dentist. She called me early this morning and asked me to walk over and keep an eye on you two." The old woman giggled. "As if you two big kids need a babysitter."

"Hey, wait a minute. Today's Saturday," said Kareem. "Dad doesn't work on Saturdays."

"I'm sure that's what your mother told me," said Mrs. Heeley.

"Morning," said Amina cheerfully, bouncing into the kitchen.

"Good morning, little one," said Mrs. Heeley.

Amina whispered to Kareem, "So did you enjoy eating all the cupcakes when no one was around?"

Kareem leaned toward her and said, "Disappointed I'm not a zombie?"

Amina glared at him. "You haven't eaten enough," she said. "You have to eat a lot before you change."

Kareem looked at the stout old woman in front of the stove. *I'll bet she's eaten a lot of them,* he thought. *She said they were her favorite thing to bake.*

"Why don't you go into the dining room and I'll finish making your breakfast. How does that sound?" Mrs. Heeley said.

"Great!" said Amina.

"And I'll add a few of my special ingredients," she said.

Kareem stared at her. The old woman patted his head. Kareem turned and headed into the dining room to join his sister.

"So sweet," the old woman said. She licked her lips greedily. Under her breath she mumbled, "And both of them so smart. I wonder how sweet their little brains taste?"

ABOUT THE AUTHOR

Michael Dahl, the author of the Library of Doom and Troll Hunters series, is an expert on fear. He is afraid of heights (but he still flies). He is afraid of small, enclosed spaces (but his house is crammed with over 3,000 books). He is afraid of ghosts (but that same house is haunted). He hopes that by writing about fear, he will eventually be able to overcome his own. So far it is not working. But he is afraid to stop. He claims that, if he had to, he would travel to Mount Doom in order to toss in a dangerous piece of jewelry. Even though he is afraid of volcanoes. And jewelry.

ABOUT THE ILLUSTRATOR

Xavier Bonet is an illustrator and comic-book artist who resides in Barcelona. Experienced in 2D illustration, he has worked as an animator and a background artist for several different production companies. He aims to create works full of color, texture, and sensation, using both traditional and digital tools. His work in children's literature is inspired by magic and fantasy as well as his passion for the art.

MICHAEL DAHL TELLS ALL

I read somewhere that we humans love telling stories so much that even while we sleep we keep telling them — in dreams and nightmares. Every day, my brain absorbs words and music and faces from the world and then I wrap them up with a spooky ending. I guess I was born that way, and I can't stop. Sometimes I try looking inside my mind to figure out where some of these stories come from. Here's what I've come up with for the stories in this book.

WHAT THEY FOUND IN THE ALLEY

When I was in elementary school, I lived in the heart of Minneapolis with an alley running behind our house. Across the alley was a funeral home, where friends and I would go after it rained to dig up worms in the lawn. Alleys were good short cuts when biking and also made great hiding places when we played Spies. Some alleys were long and dark, filled with trash cans, rusty back doors, boarded-up windows, and pieces of old furniture. In one alley, some friends claimed they found priceless gems that had been accidentally tossed out from our local jewelry store. I searched and searched but never found any myself. When coming up with locations for a scary story, I thought of those alleys from my childhood. Luckily nothing extraterrestrial happened to me back there — or did it?

THE CREEPING WOMAN

A horror movie I saw once had a scene where a faceless woman crawled out of a TV set! I'll never forget the sight of her long black hair hanging down and her pale white arms reaching out from the flickering screen. It still gives me shivers. I must have been thinking of her when this idea popped into my head. Why Christmas? I like scary stories that contain something, a location or an event, that is normally cheerful and bright. The happy parts make the scary parts stand out and become even scarier.

PLEASE DON'T TOUCH THE BUS DRIVER

Scientists predict that robot-controlled cars will drive us around in the future. We'll simply step inside the car, tell the robot where we want to go, and then take a nap as we're whisked off to our location. But what if something goes wrong? That's what worries me about them. What if we end up in the wrong place, or the robot breaks down? And what if the robot doesn't look like a robot, but like a human instead? Could these robo-cars be here already and nobody has told us? Whenever I ride a bus or taxicab I stay wide-awake, because you never know . . .

ROLLER GHOSTER

My friends Christianne and Eliza suggested that I write a story about a haunted roller coaster. Roller coasters are already scary to those of us who don't like heights or moving too fast. I loved the idea, but I didn't want the ghost, or ghosts, to seem too obvious. Plus, I wanted the reader to be surprised by the ending. Hopefully that's what happened when you read this story.

MOTHER WHO

When I was quite young, I was frightened of getting lost in the grocery store. Around the same time, about age seven, I saw the original version of the movie *Invaders from Mars*. In the movie, the eleven-year-old hero learns that Martians have turned his parents into zombies. They're not his parents anymore! Nothing seemed more terrifying to my younger self. I hoped that by combining these two fears — getting lost in a store and unreal parents — the tale would be twice as creepy.

ZOMBIE CUPCAKES

As with the "The Creeping Woman" story, I like mixing up funny and scary things. Zombies are everywhere these days, in comics and on television and in films. Almost anything can become a zombie: grown-ups, kids, animals. I tried imagining something completely different from the normal walking dead guy. Something harmless and sweet. Cupcakes. Then I thought of that old saying, "You are what you eat." Which means that having dessert is now added to the list of things that frighten me.

GLOSSARY

aquarium (uh-KWAIR-ee-uhm) — a glass tank in which you can keep fish

breadbox (BRED-boks) — a container for storing bread and other baked goods

invasion (in-VAY-shuhn) — an act of invading, especially when an army enters another territory

legend (LEJ-uhnd) — a story handed down from earlier times, often based on facts but not entirely true

loudspeaker (LOUD-spee-kur) — a machine that makes sounds loud enough to be heard in a large room or area

mismatched (mis-MACHT) — not matching correctly

ogre (OH-gur) — a cruel giant or monster in stories that eats humans beings

phase (FAZE) — a step in a series of actions

portal (POR-tuhl) — an entrance, especially an important one

realm (RELM) — a kingdom

replacement (ri-PLASE-muhnt) — one thing that takes the place of another

routine (roo-TEEN) — a regular series of actions or way of doing things

surveying (sur-VAY-ing) — examining something carefully

triumphant (trye-UHM-fuhnt) — having won a contest

versions (VUR-zhuhns) — different or changed forms of something

DISCUSSION QUESTIONS

1. In "Mother Who," what is the connection between Mia's choice of cereal and what happens at the end of the story? Discuss the possibilities.

2. Can you explain why Ricky and Oscar showed up in the photo at the end of "Roller Ghoster"? What details in the text support your explanation?

3. How would the story "What They Found in the Alley" be different if Chip had narrated it? How would it be different if Mr. Salah had been the narrator?

WRITING PROMPTS

1. Write a summary or review of the story "Zombie Cupcakes," without giving away the ending. Explain who might like to read this story and why.

2. Describe the main characters in "Please Don't Touch the Bus Driver" in a few sentences. What details from the story support your descriptions of these characters?

3. In "The Creeping Woman," Jawan's sister Shonda heard about a woman who had been creeping into people's houses on the nightly news. Write the newscast about the creeping woman, using descriptions from the story to help.

MICHAEL DAHL'S
REALLY SCARY STORIES